S0-BDM-449

A Necklace of Raindrops

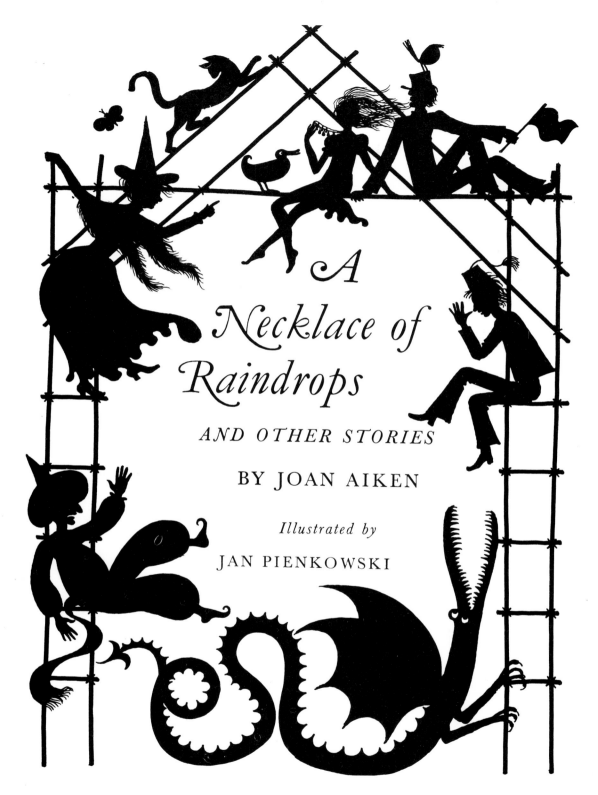

A Necklace of Raindrops

AND OTHER STORIES

BY JOAN AIKEN

Illustrated by

JAN PIENKOWSKI

JONATHAN CAPE LONDON

FIRST PUBLISHED 1968
REPRINTED 1969, 1971, 1973, 1976, 1980, 1991
© 1968 BY JOAN AIKEN
ILLUSTRATIONS © JONATHAN CAPE LTD, 1968
JONATHAN CAPE LTD, 20 VAUXHALL BRIDGE ROAD, LONDON, SW1V 2SA
ISBN 0 224 61462 2

Printed and bound in Great Britain by
Butler & Tanner Ltd, Frome, Somerset

Contents

FOR JEREMY AND MARIANNE

A Necklace of Raindrops

A man called Mr Jones and his wife lived near the sea. One stormy night Mr Jones was in his garden when he saw the holly tree by his gate begin to toss and shake.

A voice cried, "Help me! I'm stuck in the tree! Help me, or the storm will go on all night."

Very surprised, Mr Jones walked down to the tree. In the middle of it was a tall man with a long grey cloak, and a long grey beard, and the brightest eyes you ever saw.

"Who are you?" Mr Jones said. 'What are you doing in my holly tree?"

"I got stuck in it, can't you see? Help me out, or the storm will go on all night. I am the North Wind, and it is my job to blow the storm away."

So Mr Jones helped the North Wind out of the holly tree. The North Wind's hands were as cold as ice.

"Thank you," said the North Wind. "My cloak is torn, but never mind. You have helped me, so now I will do something for you."

"I don't need anything," Mr Jones said. "My wife and I have a baby girl, just born, and we are as happy as any two people in the world."

"In that case," said the North Wind, "I will be the baby's godfather. My birthday present to her will be this necklace of raindrops."

From under his grey cloak he pulled out a fine, fine silver chain. On the chain were three bright, shining drops.

"You must put it round the baby's neck," he said. "The raindrops will not wet her, and they will not come off. Every year, on her birthday, I will bring her another drop. When she has four drops she will stay dry, even if she goes out in the hardest rainstorm. And when she has five drops no thunder or lightning can harm her. And when she has six drops she will not be blown away, even by the strongest wind. And when she has seven raindrops she will be able to swim the deepest river. And when she has eight raindrops she will be able to swim the widest sea. And when she has nine raindrops she will be able to make the rain stop raining if she claps her hands. And when she has ten raindrops she will be able to make it start raining if she blows her nose."

"Stop, stop!" cried Mr Jones. "That is quite enough for one little girl!"

"I was going to stop anyway," said the North Wind. "Mind, she must never take the chain off, or it might bring bad luck. I must be off, now, to blow away the storm. I shall be back on her next birth-day, with the fourth raindrop."

And he flew away up into the sky, pushing the clouds before him so that the moon and stars could shine out.

Mr Jones went into his house and put the chain with the three raindrops round the neck of the baby, who was called Laura.

A year soon went by, and when the North Wind came back to the little house by the sea, Laura was able to crawl about, and to play with her three bright, shining raindrops. But she never took the chain off.

When the North Wind had given Laura her fourth raindrop she could not get wet, even if she was out in the hardest rain. Her mother would put her out in the garden in her pram, and people passing on the road would say, "Look at that poor little baby, left out in all this rain. She will catch cold!"

But little Laura was quite dry, and quite happy, playing with the raindrops and waving to her godfather the North Wind as he flew over.

Next year he brought her her fifth raindrop. And the year after that, the sixth. And the year after that, the seventh. Now Laura could not be harmed by the worst storm, and if she fell into a pond or river she floated like a feather. And when she had eight raindrops she was able to swim across the widest sea – but as she was happy at home she had never tried.

And when she had nine raindrops Laura found that she could make the rain stop, by clapping her hands. So there were many, many sunny days by the sea. But Laura did not always clap her hands when it rained, for she loved to see the silver drops come sliding out of the sky.

Now it was time for Laura to go to school. You can guess how the other children loved her! They would call, "Laura, Laura, make it stop raining, please, so that we can go out to play."

And Laura always made the rain stop for them.

But there was a girl called Meg who said to herself, "It isn't fair. Why should Laura have that lovely necklace and be able to stop the rain? Why shouldn't I have it?"

So Meg went to the teacher and said,

"Laura is wearing a necklace."

Then the teacher said to Laura, "You must take your necklace off in school, dear. That is the rule."

"But it will bring bad luck if I take it off," said Laura.

"Of course it will not bring bad luck. I will put it in a box for you and keep it safe till after school."

So the teacher put the necklace in a box.

But Meg saw where she put it. And when the children were out playing, and the teacher was having her dinner, Meg went quickly and took the necklace and put it in her pocket.

When the teacher found that the necklace was gone, she was very angry and sad.

"Who has taken Laura's necklace?" she asked.

But nobody answered.

Meg kept her hand tight in her pocket, holding the necklace.

And poor Laura cried all the way

home. Her tears rolled down her cheeks like rain as she walked along by the sea.

"Oh," she cried, "what will happen when I tell my godfather that I have lost his present?"

A fish put his head out of the water and said, "Don't cry, Laura dear. You put me back in the sea when a wave threw me on the sand. I will help you find your necklace."

And a bird flew down and called, "Don't cry, Laura dear. You saved me when a storm blew me on to your roof and hurt my wing. I will help you find your necklace."

And a mouse popped his head out of a hole and said, "Don't cry, Laura dear. You saved me once when I fell in the river. I will help you find your necklace."

So Laura dried her eyes. "How will you help me?" she asked.

"I will look under the sea," said the fish. "And I will ask my brothers to help me."

"I will fly about and look in the fields and woods and roads," said the bird. "And I will ask all my brothers to help me."

"I will look in the houses," said the mouse. "And I will ask my brothers to look in every corner and closet of every room in the world."

So they set to work.

While Laura was talking to her three friends, what was Meg doing?

She put on the necklace and walked out in a rainstorm. But the rain made her very wet! And when she clapped her hands to stop it raining, the rain took no notice. It rained harder than ever.

The necklace would only work for its true owner.

So Meg was angry. But she still wore the necklace, until her father saw her with it on.

"Where did you get that necklace?" he asked.

"I found it in the road," Meg said.

Which was not true!

"It is too good for a child," her father said. And he took it away from her. Meg and her father did not know that a little mouse could see them from a hole in the wall.

The mouse ran to tell his friends that the necklace was in Meg's house. And ten more mice came back with him to drag it away. But when they got there, the necklace was gone. Meg's father had sold it, for a great deal of money, to a silversmith. Two days later, a little mouse saw it in the silversmith's shop, and ran to tell his friends. But before the mice could come to take it, the silversmith had sold it to a trader who was buying fine and rare presents for the birthday of the Princess of Arabia.

Then a bird saw the necklace and flew to tell Laura.

"The necklace is on a ship, which is sailing across the sea to Arabia."

"We will follow the ship," said the

fishes. "We will tell you which way it goes. Follow us!"

But Laura stood on the edge of the sea.

"How can I swim all that way without my necklace?" she cried.

"I will take you on my back," said a dolphin. "You have often thrown me good things to eat when I was hungry."

So the dolphin took her on his back, and the fishes went on in front, and the birds flew above, and after many days they came to Arabia.

"Now where is the necklace?" called the fishes to the birds.

"The King of Arabia has it. He is going to give it to the Princess for her birthday tomorrow."

"Tomorrow is my birthday too," said Laura. "Oh, what will my godfather say when he comes to give me my tenth raindrop and finds that I have not got the necklace?"

The birds led Laura into the King's garden. And she slept all night under a palm tree. The grass was all dry, and the flowers were all brown, because it was so hot, and had not rained for a year.

Next morning the Princess came into the garden to open her presents. She had many lovely things: a flower that could sing, and a cage full of birds with green and silver feathers; a book that she could read for ever because it had no last page, and a cat who could play cat's cradle; a silver dress of spiderwebs and a gold dress of goldfish scales; a clock with a real cuckoo to tell the time, and a boat made out of a great pink shell. And among all

the other presents was Laura's necklace.

When Laura saw the necklace she ran out from under the palm tree and cried, "Oh, please, that necklace is mine!"

The King of Arabia was angry. "Who is this girl?" he said. "Who let her into my garden? Take her away and drop her in the sea!"

But the Princess, who was small and pretty, said, "Wait a minute, Papa," and to Laura she said, "How do you know it is your necklace?"

"Because my godfather gave it to me! When I am wearing it I can go out in the rain without getting wet, no storm can harm me, I can swim any river and any sea, and I can make the rain stop raining."

"But can you make it start to rain?" said the King.

"Not yet," said Laura. "Not till my godfather gives me the tenth raindrop."

"If you can make it rain you shall have the necklace," said the King. "For we badly need rain in this country."

But Laura was sad because she could not make it rain till she had her tenth raindrop.

Just then North Wind came flying into the King's garden.

"There you are, god-daughter!" he said. "I have been looking all over the world for you, to give you your birthday present. Where is your necklace?"

"The Princess has it," said poor Laura.

Then the North Wind was angry. "You should not have taken it off!" he said. And he dropped the raindrop on to the dry grass, where it was lost. Then he flew away. Laura started to cry.

"Don't cry," said the kind little Princess. "You shall have the necklace back, for I can see it is yours." And she put the chain over Laura's head. As soon as she did so, one of Laura's tears ran down and hung on the necklace beside the nine raindrops, making ten. Laura started to smile, she dried her eyes and blew her nose. And, guess what! as soon as she blew her nose, the rain began falling! It rained and it rained, the trees all spread out their leaves, and the flowers stretched their petals, they were so happy to have a drink.

At last Laura clapped her hands to stop the rain.

The King of Arabia was very pleased. "That is the finest necklace I have ever seen," he said. "Will you come and stay with us every year, so that we have enough rain?" And Laura said she would do this.

Then they sent her home in the Princess's boat, made out of a pink shell. And the birds flew overhead, and the fishes swam in front.

"I am happy to have my necklace back," said Laura. "But I am even happier to have so many friends."

. What happened to Meg? The mice told the North Wind that she had taken Laura's necklace. And he came and blew the roof off her house and let in the rain, so she was SOAKING WET!

The Cat Sat on the Mat

The cat sat on the mat. Lots of cats do that, everybody knows. And nothing strange comes of it. But once a cat sat on a mat and something strange did come of it.

This is how it all began.

There was once a little girl called Emma Pippin. She had red rosy cheeks and brown hair and she lived with her Aunt Lou. They were very poor, too poor to buy a house, so they lived in an old bus. The engine would not go, but it was a nice old bus and they loved it. The outside of the bus was painted blue, the inside was painted white, and the windows had orange curtains. There was a stove, which kept them warm, and the smoke went out of a chimney in the roof.

Look at the picture and you'll see what the bus was like.

It stood by a high, white wall. Inside this wall were many lovely green apple trees, on which were growing many lovely red apples. The apple trees were owned by a proud, grand man called Sir Laxton Superb.

Every day Aunt Lou went through a door into the orchard to work for Sir Laxton Superb. Aunt Lou picked the apples, which were sent away to shops. There were so many trees that when Aunt Lou had finished picking the last tree, the first one had apples growing on it again!

But Aunt Lou could not take any lovely red apples for herself. Not a single one! Sir Laxton Superb was a very mean man. He only let her take the apples that were going bad. And he only paid her a penny a day.

As for Emma, she might not even go into the orchard. She longed to go in, for Aunt Lou had told her about the green trees and the red apples, but Sir Laxton Superb said children would eat his apples, or spoil them. So Emma had to stay outside, looking at the high white wall.

She had no toys to play with. She and Aunt Lou were too poor. So she worked hard all day keeping the bus nice and clean. And she cooked dinner, ready for when Aunt Lou came home.

What did she cook? Bad apples! She made bad-apple sauce, bad-apple cake, bad-apple pie, even bad-toffee-apples.

Emma was growing very fast. Every day she grew taller. She grew so fast that she was growing too big for her dress. And Aunt Lou was to poor to buy her a new dress. Emma's dress was so small that she could hardly move!

"If we take your dress off to wash it," Aunt Lou said, "we may not be able to get it back on again. I shall wash you and your dress both together."

So she put Emma in the bath, and she washed Emma and the dress, and hung them both on the clothes-line to dry.

Then Aunt Lou went off for the day to pick apples. "You may get down when you and your dress are dry," she said.

As Emma was swinging in the wind, a poor old fairy came along. She walked slowly with a stick, because she was so old.

When she saw Emma, swinging on the clothes-line, she started to laugh. She laughed and she laughed! She laughed so much she nearly fell over!

"Oh!" she said, when she could stop laughing. "I have never seen anyone on a clothes-line before. You can't think how funny you look!"

Emma said, "My dress is too small, so Aunt Lou washes it on me, in case I can't put it on again when I have taken it off. I'm almost dry now, so I can come down if you will help me."

The fairy helped Emma down.

"Would you like to

come into our bus," Emma said, "and have some bad-apple cake?"

"Thank you," said the fairy. "I should like to very much. I have never been in a bus."

The fairy thought the bus was lovely. And she had three helpings of bad-apple cake. She said it was very good! She told Emma,

"You have cheered me up, so I shall try to help you. I am too old and poor to give you a grand present, but I will give you three of my dresses. They are too small for me now, but they will be just right for you."

So the fairy gave Emma three dresses, one red, one blue, and one grey.

"And as well as the dresses," she said, "I will give you a kitten to play with."

The kitten was called Sam, and he was black, with green eyes. Emma loved him at once, because he was so small and soft and bouncy.

Then the fairy said goodbye and

walked slowly away with her stick.

Aunt Lou was very pleased when she came home and saw the dresses. She cut up the red one and the blue one, and made new dresses for Emma. They looked lovely. Aunt Lou left the grey dress, because it was not a pretty colour.

Emma had the red dress for weekdays and the blue dress for Sundays.

As for Sam – he slept on Emma's bed every night!

"After all," Emma said to Aunt Lou, "he *is* a fairy cat."

"Fairy cat or no fairy cat," said Aunt Lou, "he has very muddy paws!"

Every night Sam left black BLACK footprints all over Emma's nice clean bed. On her sheets! And on her blankets! And on her pillow!

So Emma made a grey mat from the fairy's grey dress, and put it on her bed. And Sam jumped on to it. But on his way he walked over the pillow and left BLACK footmarks before sitting on the mat.

"Oh dear, Sam," said Emma. "You should clean your feet on your mat. I *wish* you would. What will Aunt Lou say when she comes home and sees those black marks?"

When Emma said, "I *wish* you would," Sam stood up. He looked at Emma. Then he wiped his feet on the mat! Emma *was* surprised.

"Why!" she said. "It must be a wishing-mat. What else can I wish? I wish those black, muddy marks were not on my pillow."

That very minute, Emma's pillow was clean as clean. The black marks had gone.

"Now," Emma said, "I wish I had a big meat pie and some ice-cream for Aunt Lou's dinner when she comes home."

Just as Emma said this, Sam got up. And as Emma said the word *ice*, Sam jumped off his mat.

When Emma looked on the kitchen table, there was a big meat pie and a lump of ice.

"I wished for ice-cream, not ice," said Emma. "I wish the ice would turn into ice-cream."

But the ice did not turn into ice-cream.

"I know," Emma said. "The mat is only a wishing-mat when Sam is sitting on it. Please, Sam, will you get back on your mat?"

But Sam wanted to go out, and he jumped out of the window.

"I will wish for more things when Sam comes back," Emma said.

But Aunt Lou came back before Sam.

Aunt Lou was cross, because Sir Laxton Superb had told her he did not want her shabby old bus standing by his nice white wall.

"You will have to move it to some other place," he said.

So Aunt Lou was worried. Where could they move their bus? Who could they get to help them? They were too poor to pay anybody. Aunt Lou was tired and sad, so she did not listen to what

Emma was telling her.

"Aunt Lou, I've got a wishing-mat," Emma said.

"Yes, dear," Aunt Lou said, but she was not really listening.

"It gives wishes!" Emma said.

"Yes, dear," Aunt Lou said, but she was not really listening.

"It cleaned my bed. And it gave us this nice meat pie!"

"Yes, dear." But Aunt Lou did not really hear what Emma was saying. She ate some pie, but she was worrying so much about how to move the bus that she never even tasted it. She might just as well have been eating bad-apple sauce!

Aunt Lou did not tell Emma that they had to move the bus.

Grown-ups do not always tell their troubles to children, but sometimes it would be better if they did.

Sam didn't come home all night. He went into the woods and played puss-in-the-corner with the squirrels. By the time he came home, Aunt Lou had gone off to pick apples.

Sam jumped up on to his mat. Emma had been waiting for this.

"I wish I had a toy!" she said. "A skipping-rope! And some balloons! And a ball! And a pair of skates! And a box of—"

Just then Sam jumped off his mat again. A big red ball had rolled across the floor and he wanted to chase it.

All the things were there that Emma had wished for. The skipping-rope. And the balloons. And the ball. And the skates.

Emma had been going to wish for a box of paints, but Sam jumped off the mat before she had finished. So all she got was a big empty box. She put the skates in it.

Emma had a very happy morning. She skipped and skipped and skipped. Then she skated and skated and skated. Then she played with the ball. Sam played with her. Then she played with the balloons. Sam did too. This was not good for the balloons.

At last Sam and Emma were both tired. Sam went to sleep on his mat.

"I wish I had a paint-box!" said Emma.

At once there was a big, lovely paint-box on the table in the bus. There were many colours in it – red, blue, green, yellow, orange, purple – all the colours you can think of!

"Oh, what lovely paints!" Emma said. "I shall paint a fine picture. I should like to paint the best picture in the whole world."

Emma looked for a bit of paper. But none of the bits of paper in the bus was big enough for the picture she wanted to paint.

"I know!" she said. "I'll paint a picture on the white wall."

So she started painting a picture on Sir Laxton Superb's high white wall. First she painted all the part she could reach. Then she climbed on a chair and painted all the high-up part of the wall.

What did Emma paint?

She painted a picture of the orchard inside the wall – the green, green trees and the red, red apples. But as she had never seen it, she painted the apples many other colours as well – pink and yellow and blue and gold and orange. Under the trees she painted foxes and squirrels and rabbits, eating bread and jelly. Birds were flying through the air, playing with balloons. Dogs were skating. Cats were skipping.

It was a very fine picture – the finest in the whole world.

And all the time, Sam went on sleeping on his mat. He was tired out.

Then Aunt Lou came through the door in the wall.

"Look, Aunt Lou!" Emma called. "Look at the lovely picture I've painted!"

But after Aunt Lou came Sir Laxton Superb.

"You must move your bus away at the end of this week!" Sir Laxton Superb was saying.

And all the time, Sam was sleeping on his mat.

Aunt Lou looked very worried. When Emma said, "Look at my lovely picture," she said, "Yes, dear," without looking. But Sir Laxton Superb looked. And his face went red – redder than the reddest apple you ever saw!

"*What* have you done to my lovely white wall?" he said. He looked so cross that Emma thought he might go off bang like a balloon.

"I've painted the best picture in the whole world on it," she said. "Aren't you pleased?"

But Sir Laxton Superb was not pleased. Not at all pleased!

"You must rub it all off again!" he said. "And you must leave *at once!* Today! This minute!"

Aunt Lou began to cry. "But where can we go?" she said.

"I don't care!" Sir Laxton Superb said. (And Sam was still sleeping on his mat.) "I wish the wind would blow you and your shabby old bus up into the sky!"

And Sam was *still* asleep on his mat!

That very minute a great wind blew Aunt Lou, and Emma, and the bus, up into the air. Up they went, up, up, and up, till they landed on a fat white cloud. All the things in the bus fell about, but nothing broke. And, just think, Sam was still asleep on his mat. He was so tired after all those games.

"Well!" said Aunt Lou. "I thought of living in plenty of places, but I never thought of living up in the sky! What shall we find to eat up here?"

"That's easy," Emma said. And she wished for a roast chicken, and a big iced cake, and a jug of milk, and an orange jelly.

For Sam was still asleep on his mat!

After dinner they walked about on the cloud. It was soft – just like the hay in a hay barn. And they found lots of apples – because the wind had blown all the

apples off Sir Laxton Superb's trees. They were rolling about, all over the sky!

From that day, the trees in Sir Laxton Superb's orchard never had any more apples. And although he tried to rub Emma's picture off the wall, he couldn't.

"If Sam's mat is a wishing-mat," Aunt Lou said, "we could wish our bus to be moved to California. Or Canada. Or Canton. Or the Canary Islands."

"Oh, no!" said Emma. "Let's go on living up here."

And so they did. If you look up some dark night you may get a sight of the old bus shining away up there. And you are almost sure to see some of the apples.

There's some Sky in this Pie

There was an old man and an old woman, and they lived in a very cold country. One winter day the old man said to the old woman,

"My dear, it is so cold, I should like it very much if you would make a good, hot apple pie."

And the old woman said, "Yes, my dear, I will make an apple pie."

So she took sugar, and she took spices, and she took apples, and she put them in a pie-dish. Then she took flour, and she took fat, and she took water, and she began to make pastry to cover the pie. First she rubbed the fat into the flour, then she made it into a lump with a little water.

Then she took a roller and began to roll out the pastry.

While she was doing this, the old man said, "Look out of the window, my dear, see, it is beginning to snow."

And the old woman looked out of the window at the snow, coming down so fast out of the white sky.

Then she went on rolling the pastry. But what do you think happened? A little corner of the sky that she had been looking at got caught in the pastry. And that little bit of sky was pulled under the roller, just the way a shirt is pulled into the wringer. So when the old woman rolled her pastry flat and put it on the pie-dish, there was a piece of sky in it! But the old woman did not know this. She put the pie in the oven, and soon it began to smell very good.

"Is it dinner time yet?" said the old man.

"Soon," said the old woman. She put spoons and forks and plates on the table.

"Is it dinner time now?" said the old man.

"Yes," said the old woman, and she opened the oven door.

But what do you think? That pie was so light, because of the bit of sky in it, that

it floated out of the oven, right across the room.

"Stop it, stop it!" cried the old woman. She made a grab, and he made a grab, but the pie floated out of the door, and they ran after it into the garden.

"Jump on it!" cried the old man. So he jumped on it, and she jumped on it.

But the pie was so light that it carried them up into the air, through the snow-flakes falling out of the white sky.

Their little black-and-white cat Whisky was in the apple tree, looking at the snow.

"Stop us, stop us!" they called to Whisky. So he jumped on to the pie. But he was too light to stop it, and still it went floating on through the falling snow. They went higher and higher. The birds called to them:

"Old woman, old man, little puss, so high,
Sailing along on your apple pie,
Why are you floating across the sky?"

And the old woman answered,

"Because we can't stop, that's the reason
  why."

They went on, and they came to a
plane that had run out of fuel. So there it
was, stuck, in the middle of the sky. And
the airman was inside, and he was very
cold. He called out,

"Old woman, old man, little puss, so high,
Sailing along on your apple pie,
Why are you floating across the sky?"

And the old woman answered,

"Because we can't stop, that's the reason
why."

"May I come with you?" called the
airman.
"Yes, of course you may."
So he jumped on the pie and went
floating along with them.
They went a little farther and they saw
a duck who had forgotten how to fly. So

there it was in the middle of a cloud. And
the duck called,

"Old woman, old man, little puss, and
    airman, so high,
Sailing along on your apple pie,
Why are you floating across the sky?"

And the old woman answered,

"Because we can't stop, that's the reason
    why."

"May I come with you?"

"Yes, of course you may."

So the duck jumped on the pie and went floating along with them.

They went a little farther and they passed a tall mountain. On the tip-top of the mountain was a mountain goat, who had forgotten the way down. So he called to them,

"Old woman, old man, little puss, and
    airman, and duck, so high,
Sailing along on your apple pie,
Why are you floating across the sky?"

And the old woman answered,

"Because we can't stop, that's the reason why."

"May I come with you?"

"Yes, of course you may."

So the goat jumped on the pie too.

Then they went a little farther and they came to a big city with high, high buildings. And on top of one of the buildings

was a sad, cross, homesick elephant, looking sadly and crossly at the snow. She
called to them,

"Old woman, old man, little puss, and
    airman, and duck, and goat, so high,
Sailing along on your apple pie,
Why are you floating across the sky?"

And the old woman answered,

"Because we can't stop, that's the reason
    why."

"Your pie smells so warm and spicy, it
makes me think of my homeland," said
the elephant. "May I come with you?"
"Yes, of course you may."
So the elephant jumped on to the pie
and they went floating on. But the
elephant was so heavy that she made the
pie tip to one side.
Now as they floated on, by and by they
left the cold and the snow behind, and
came to where it was warm. Down below
was the blue, blue sea, and in the blue sea

were many little islands with white sand and green trees.

By this time the pie was beginning to cool off, and as it cooled it went down and down.

"Let us land on one of these lovely islands," said the old man. "They have white sand and green trees, and ever so many flowers."

"Yes, let us!" said the old woman, and Whisky the cat, and the duck, and the mountain goat, and the airman, and the elephant.

But the people on the island saw them coming and put up a big sign that said NO PARKING FOR PIES.

So they went a little farther and they came to another island. But the people on that island also put up a big sign that said NO PARKING FOR PIES.

"Oh dear," said the old woman, "will no one let us land?"

By this time the pie was so cool that it sank down on the sea.

"Now we are all right," said the old man. "Our own pie makes a very fine island."

"There are no trees!" said the old woman. "There are no flowers! And what shall we eat, and what shall we drink?"

But the sun was so warm that fine apple trees soon grew up, with green leaves, and pink flowers, and red apples. And the mountain goat gave them milk, and the duck gave them eggs, and Whisky the cat caught fish in the sea. And the elephant picked apples for them off the trees with her trunk.

So they lived happily on the island and never went home again.

And all this happened because the old woman baked a bit of sky in her pie!

The Elves in the Shelves

There was a little girl called Janet, and it was her birthday. She had lots of presents. A little red bicycle. And a pair of roller-skates. And a skipping-rope. And a big pile of books. But just the same, Janet was not very happy.

Why? Because her mother was away, visiting her sick granny. And her daddy, who was a train driver, had to go off and drive his train. And so Janet would be all alone that night.

Her daddy gave her a very nice supper – bread and butter and brown sugar and a drink of creamy milk. Then he tucked her up in bed and said, "Shut your eyes and go to sleep, and in no time at all it will be tomorrow and I shall be home for breakfast." Off he went to drive his train.

Janet shut her eyes, but then she opened them again. She did not like being all alone.

"Oh," sighed Janet, "I wish I had someone to talk to."

Then she heard a queer noise. What could it be?

Pitter-patter, tip-tap, scuffle-scuffle, rattle-rattle, pitter-patter. Janet listened. The noise came from the next room. There it was again! Pitter-patter, tip-tap, scuffle-scuffle, rattle-rattle, pitter-patter. Janet jumped out of bed and tiptoed to the next room.

What do you think she saw?

All her new books were opening, and all the creatures in them were coming out. There was a book about elves, and all the elves were running out of the book and playing leap-frog and climbing up into the china closet. There was a book about mermaids, and all the mermaids were swimming out and diving into the bath. There was a book about penguins, and all the penguins were waddling out and climbing up into the ice-box. There was a book about seals, and all the seals were

flopping out and pulling each other up
into the sink.

    So when Janet looked, she saw

elves in the shelves,
   mermaids in the bathtub,
     penguins in the ice-box,
      rabbits in the coal-bin,
       peacocks on the table and
      seals in the sink.

Wasn't that a funny sight, enough to make you blink!

"*Who* are all of you?" said Janet. "And *what* are you doing here?"

"We have come to play with you, so you shan't be all alone!"

Janet had never had so many playmates before. Who should she play with first? The elves in the shelves? They were playing football with a marble. Or the mermaids in the bathtub? They were floating on Janet's sponge for a raft. Or the penguins in the ice-box? They were sliding on a slippery bit of ice. Or the rabbits in the coal-bin? They were playing hunt-the-thimble. Or the peacocks on the table? They were playing patience. Or the seals in the sink? They were playing splashing.

First Janet played with the elves. Then with the mermaids. Then with the penguins. Then with the rabbits. Then with the peacocks. Then with the seals.

Then she heard a voice behind her. It

said, "Nobody wants to play with *me!*"

Janet looked round. There stood a tiger in front of the fire. He had come out of the very bottom book of all. He was big, and he had long, long whiskers and a long, long tail, and he had black and yellow stripes all over.

"Tickle my tail!" he said, " and I'll chase you!"

"We don't like to be chased," cried the elves. "You're too rough." But he chased the elves along the shelves.

"We don't like to be chased," cried the mermaids. But Tiger chased them out of the bathtub.

"We don't want to be chased," cried the penguins. But Tiger chased them out of the ice-box.

"We don't want to be chased," squeaked the rabbits. But Tiger chased them out of the coal-bin.

"We don't want to be chased," barked the seals. But Tiger chased them out of the sink.

"We don't want to be chased," screamed the peacocks. But Tiger chased them off the table.

Everyone was cross, and some of the elves were crying.

"Tiger," said Janet, "you are too rough. You must play more gently."

"Tell him to go back into his book!" everybody cried.

So Janet picked up the book and said, "Bad boy! Bad Tiger! Go back inside!" Tiger looked sad. "I only want to run," he said. "For I can run

faster than the wind,
   faster than the weather,
      faster than the fastest clouds
         that cross the sky together!

"Please," Tiger said to Janet, "can I go for a run outside? After that I will be quiet and good, and not chase the others."

"I had better come too," Janet said, "to keep an eye on you."

"Then jump on my back and tickle my tail!"

So Janet jumped on his back and tickled his tail. And he ran out of the door and down the stairs and along the street and across the park, fast, faster, fastest of all! And as he ran he sang,

"I can run
    faster than the wind,
        faster than the weather,
            faster than the fastest clouds
                that cross the sky together."

Then they met a man with a glass foot. He cried,

"Oh, please, my hat has blown off. Can you catch it for me, for if I run I might break my glass foot."

"Pooh!" said Tiger. "I can easily catch your hat."

And he went *chasing* across the park and they caught the hat and gave it back to the man with the glass foot. And he was very grateful.

Then they saw a woman who called,
"Please, can you help me? I belong in
Tomorrow, but I got left behind. Can
you catch up with Tomorrow for me?"

"Easy," said Tiger. "For I can run

faster than the wind,
   faster than the weather,
      faster than the fastest clouds
         that cross the sky together.

Jump on my back behind Janet and tickle
my tail."

So the woman jumped on his back and
she tickled his tail. And he went *chasing*

56

over the country and easily caught up
with Tomorrow and put the woman back
where she belonged.

"Thank you," she called. "I'll send
you a postcard from Tomorrow."

Then they saw a boy who called,
"Help! A Pandaconda from the circus is
chasing me because I pulled its whiskers.
Save me!"

"Easy!" said Tiger. "Jump on my
back and tickle my tail."

So they tickled his tail and away he

went, fast, faster, fastest of all! At first the Pandaconda came whistling after, but soon it gave up and went back to sleep in its hole under the merry-go-round.

"Thank you for saving me," said the boy. And he gave them each a nut and jumped off as they passed by his home.

Then Janet said, "*Goodness*, there's the train that my daddy comes home on. Quick, quick, or he'll be home first and wonder where I am!"

"Easy!" said Tiger. "I can beat a train any day. For I can run

faster than the wind,
　　faster than the weather,
　　　　faster than the fastest clouds
　　　　　　that cross the sky together.

Only tickle my tail." So Janet tickled his tail and they went *racing* back, over the country and over the town, over houses and churches and mountains and rivers, across the park and along the street, and in at Janet's window.

"Quick!" she cried. "You must all get into your books, for my daddy's coming home."

For there were

elves in the shelves,
mermaids in the bathtub,
penguins in the ice-box,
rabbits in the coal-bin,
peacocks on the table and
seals in the sink.

"I will play with you all again tomorrow night," Janet promised. She pushed them all into their books (Tiger was the hardest to push because he was so big) and then she ran next door and jumped into bed and shut her eyes tight.

Next thing, she was asleep!

And next thing she was awake again, and there was her daddy making breakfast. After breakfast, Janet went and looked at her books, but they were quite quiet and still. If it hadn't been for a small, just the *smallest* footprint on a shelf, a little,

just the *littlest* gold scale in the bathtub,
a tiny, just the *tiniest* feather in the ice-box,
and ONE tiger's whisker on the rug, you
would never have guessed that there had
been

elves in the shelves,
    mermaids in the bathtub,
        penguins in the ice-box,
            rabbits in the coal-bin,
                peacocks on the table,
                seals in the sink

and a big stripy tiger sitting in front of
the fire . . .

The Three Travellers

There was once a little tiny station in the middle of a huge desert. On either side of it the sand stretched away as far as the eye could see, and much farther too, and beyond the sand lay prairie, and beyond the prairie were valleys and mountains, and through all these lands the railway ran in both directions, on and on, gracious knows where.

The station's name was Desert. There was just one building and three men lived in it: Mr Smith the signalman, and Mr Jones the porter, and Mr Brown the ticket-collector.

You may think it odd that there were three men to look after one tiny station, but the people who ran the railway knew that if you left two men together in a lonely place they would quarrel, but if you left three men, two of them could always grumble to each other about the third, and then they would be quite happy.

These three men were happy enough, for they had no wives to worry about the desert dust, and no children to pester them for stories or piggy-backs, but they weren't *completely* happy and this is why:

Every day huge roaring trains would thunder across the desert, from west to east and from east to west, getting bigger and bigger as they neared the station, and smaller and smaller as they rushed away from it, but they never stopped.

Nobody ever wanted to get off at Desert.

"Oh, if only I could use my signals once in a while," mourned Mr Smith. "I oil them and polish them every day, but not once in the last fifteen years have I had a chance to pull the lever and signal a train to stop. It breaks a man's heart, it does!"

"Oh, if only I could clip a ticket once in a while," sighed Mr Brown. "I keep my clippers shining and bright, but what's the use? Not once in fifteen years have I had a chance to punch with them. A man's talents rust in this place."

"Oh, if only I could carry someone's luggage once in a while," lamented Mr Jones. "In the big city stations the porters are rich from the tips people give them, but how can anyone hope to get rich here? I do my press-ups every morning to keep me strong and supple, but not once in fifteen years have I had the chance to carry so much as a hatbox. There's no chance for a man here!"

Besides this trouble there was another thing that fretted these three men. They had one day off every week – Sunday, when no trains ran either way – but there was nothing to do on it. Nowhere to go. The next stop along the line from Desert was more than a thousand miles away, and it would cost more than a week's wages to go so far. And even if you took the last train out on a Saturday night, you couldn't travel all that way and go to the

cinema, and be back by Monday morning. So on Sundays they just sat about on the station platform, and yawned, and wished it were Monday.

But one day Mr Jones counted his savings carefully and said, "Friends, your wishes are going to be granted. I have saved enough for a week's holiday. Mr Smith can signal a train to stop, and Mr Brown can clip my ticket, and I'm going to see the world, as far as the train can take me."

The other two men were wildly excited. Mr Smith spent the whole night oiling his levers, and Mr Brown selected

his thickest, squarest ticket and polished
his clippers. It was a splendid moment
next morning when the great, proud train,
instead of roaring through Desert Station,
came hissing to a stop, all for Mr Jones.

He put his own luggage on it, climbed
up, waved goodbye to his friends, and
shouted, "Back on Saturday," and off he
went to the east.

Halfway through the week they had a
postcard, dropped from a passing train,
to say he'd be back by the noon train on
Saturday, so a couple of hours before it
was due Mr Smith pulled his signal to the
"stop" position. He and Mr Brown had

spent all their spare time that week sitting under a cactus thorn and discussing what Mr Jones would have to tell them about his travels when he came back, and what presents he would bring them.

As soon as the train stopped Mr Jones jumped off it, and Mr Brown carefully took his ticket while Mr Smith signalled the train on its way again. Then they made a pot of coffee and sat down to listen to the traveller's tale.

"Brothers!" said he, "the world is a big place! The train took me through more country than I could remember in a lifetime, and ended in a city bigger than the whole of this desert. Why, the station itself was as big as a town, with shops and theatres and hotels and restaurants in it. There was even a circus, right in the station! So I never bothered to go out into the town, just stayed in the station, and I had a fine time, I can tell you. I've brought you these things."

And he carefully brought out their

presents, for Mr Smith a paperweight shaped like a skyscraper, and for Mr Brown a box with a picture of a huge, splendid station on its lid. They were very pleased.

Next week Mr Smith counted his money and said, "Brothers, you're in luck again, for I've saved enough money for my holiday and I'm going to catch the westbound train and go as far as it will go."

"But who will look after the signals?" objected Mr Jones.

"Mr Brown will; I've been teaching him all week."

So Mr Brown got out another of his best tickets for Mr Smith, and then hurried off to the signals. Mr Jones took Mr Smith's case and put it on the train (and Mr Smith gave him a handsome tip). He climbed on board, and off he went.

Next Saturday, back he came with eyes like stars. As soon as the train was on its way again, and they had made a pot of coffee, they sat down to listen to his story.

"My!" said Mr Smith. "The world is even bigger than I thought! So much country we went through, I've already forgotten half of it. But at the end of the journey we went over a range of mountains so high I thought we'd graze the moon, with pine trees like needles, and snow like a shaking of salt. Then the train went rushing down, till I was sure the brakes would fail and we'd go over a precipice. At last we came to the sea, and there we stopped. Brothers, the sea is even bigger than this desert! I brought you these things."

He had brought for Mr Brown a pearl-coloured shell, and for Mr Jones a big chunk of shining white crystal rock, and they thought these presents were very beautiful.

Then they began saying to Mr Brown: "When are you going for your holiday?" And Mr Smith said, "Go to the mountains! Go to the mountains and the sea!"

But Mr Jones said, "No, go to the city! The city is much more beautiful and fascinating." And they began to argue and shout at one another.

But Mr Brown was a very quiet man, and he thought for a long time and said, "I don't fancy going for such a long train-ride as that. I get train-sick. Besides, you've been to those places and told me what they're like. I want to go somewhere different."

"But there isn't anywhere else to go," they told him. "The railway only goes two ways, east and west."

"I shall go north," said Mr Brown, and he packed a bag, just a little one, with some bread and cheese and a bottle of beer.

"How *can* you go north?"

"Walking, on my feet," said Mr Brown, and when Sunday came he crossed the tracks and set off walking, very early in the morning.

Mr Jones and Mr Smith watched his figure going straight away from them over the brown sand, getting smaller and smaller in the distance, until he was out of sight. At first his footprints were sharp and clear, while the dew lay on the sand, and then as the sun climbed higher up the sky they gradually crumbled and sank away, as if the sand were melting like snow in the heat.

"Shall we ever see him again?" Mr Jones and Mr Smith asked each other.

But in the evening when the sun was level and low they saw a tiny dot far away coming nearer and nearer, and when it was quite close they saw that it was Mr Brown. And his eyes were shining and his face was full of joy.

"Well?" they said, when they had made a pot of coffee and sat down to drink it. "Where have you been and what have you seen?"

"Brothers," said Mr Brown, "two hours' walk away from this station I found an oasis. There's a spring of fresh water, and green grass, and flowers, and orange and lemon trees. I've brought you these presents."

He gave to Mr Jones an enormous juicy orange, and to Mr Smith a bunch of feathery leaves and blue flowers.

If you should ever find yourself in Desert Station on a Sunday, you won't be surprised to see that there is nobody at home. The three men are two hours' walk away, lying on the grass by the cool spring and listening to the birds.

On the station signboard, under DESERT, the words FOR OASIS have been added.

The Baker's Cat

Once there was an old lady, Mrs Jones, who lived with her cat, Mog. Mrs Jones kept a baker's shop, in a little tiny town, at the bottom of a valley between two mountains.

Every morning you could see Mrs Jones's light twinkle out, long before all the other houses in the town, because she got up very early to bake loaves and buns and jam tarts and Welsh cakes.

First thing in the morning Mrs Jones lit a big fire. Then she made dough, out of water and sugar and yeast. Then she put the dough into pans and set it in front of the fire to rise.

Mog got up early too. *He* got up to catch mice. When he had chased all the mice out of the bakery, he wanted to sit in front of the warm fire. But Mrs Jones wouldn't let him, because of the loaves and buns there, rising in their pans.

She said, "Don't sit on the buns, Mog."

The buns were rising nicely. They were getting fine and big. That is what yeast does. It makes bread and buns and cakes swell up and get bigger and bigger.

As Mog was not allowed to sit by the fire, he went to play in the sink.

Most cats hate water, but Mog didn't. He loved it. He liked to sit by the tap, hitting the drops with his paw as they fell, and getting water all over his whiskers!

What did Mog look like? His back, and his sides, and his legs down as far as where his socks would have come to, and his face and ears and his tail were all marmalade coloured. His stomach and his waistcoat and his paws were white. And he had a white tassel at the tip of his tail, white fringes to his ears, and white whiskers. The water made his marmalade fur go almost fox colour and his paws and waistcoat shining-white clean.

But Mrs Jones said, "Mog, you are getting too excited. You are shaking water all over my pans of buns, just when they are getting nice and big. Run along and play outside.''

Mog was affronted. He put his ears and tail down (when cats are pleased they put their ears and tails *up*) and he went out. It was raining hard.

A rushing, rocky river ran through the middle of the town. Mog went and sat *in* the water and looked for fish. But there were no fish in that part of the river. Mog got wetter and wetter. But he didn't care. Presently he began to sneeze.

Then Mrs Jones opened her door and called, ''Mog! I have put the buns in the oven. You can come in now, and sit by the fire.''

Mog was so wet that he was shiny all over, as if he had been polished. As he sat by the fire he sneezed nine times.

Mrs Jones said, ''Oh dear, Mog, are you catching a cold?''

She dried him with a towel and gave him some warm milk with yeast in it.

Yeast is good for people when they are poorly.

Then she left him sitting in front of the fire and began making jam tarts. When she had put the tarts in the oven she went out shopping, taking her umbrella.

But what do you think was happening to Mog?

The yeast was making him rise.

As he sat dozing in front of the lovely warm fire he was growing bigger and bigger.

First he grew as big as a sheep.

Then he grew as big as a donkey.

Then he grew as big as a cart-horse.

Then he grew as big as a hippopotamus.

By now he was too big for Mrs Jones's little kitchen, but he was *far* too big to get through the door. He just burst the walls.

When Mrs Jones came home with her shopping-bag and her umbrella she cried out,

"Mercy me, what is happening to my house?"

The whole house was bulging. It was swaying. Huge whiskers were poking out of the kitchen window. A marmalade-coloured tail came out of the door. A white paw came out of one bedroom window, and an ear with a white fringe out of the other.

"Morow?" said Mog. He was waking up from his nap and trying to stretch.

Then the whole house fell down.

"Oh, Mog!" cried Mrs Jones. "*Look* what you've done."

The people in the town were very astonished when they saw what had happened. They gave Mrs Jones the Town Hall to live in, because they were so fond of her (and her buns). But they were not so sure about Mog.

The Mayor said, "Suppose he goes on growing and breaks our Town Hall? Suppose he turns fierce? It would not be safe to have him in the town, he is too big."

Mrs Jones said, "Mog is a gentle cat. He would not hurt anybody."

"We will wait and see about that," said the Mayor. "Suppose he sat down on someone? Suppose he was hungry? What will he eat? He had better live outside the town, up on the mountain."

So everybody shouted, "Shoo! Scram! Pssst! Shoo!" and poor Mog was driven outside the town gates. It was still raining hard. Water was rushing down the mountains. Not that Mog cared.

But poor Mrs Jones was very sad. She began making a new lot of loaves and buns in the Town Hall, crying into them so much that the dough was too wet, and very salty.

Mog walked up the valley between the two mountains. By now he was bigger than an elephant – almost as big as a whale! When the sheep on the mountain saw him coming, they were scared to death and galloped away. But he took no notice of them. He was looking for fish in the river. He caught lots of fish! He was having a fine time.

By now it had been raining for so long that Mog heard a loud, watery roar at the top of the valley. He saw a huge wall of water coming towards him. The river was beginning to flood, as more and more rain-water poured down into it, off the mountains.

Mog thought, "If I don't stop that water, all these fine fish will be washed away."

So he sat down, plump in the middle of the valley, and he spread himself out like a big, fat cottage loaf.

The water could not get by.

The people in the town had heard the roar of the flood-water. They were very frightened. The Mayor shouted, "Run up the mountains before the water gets to the town, or we shall all be drowned!"

So they all rushed up the mountains, some on one side of the town, some on the other.

What did they see then?

Why, Mog, sitting in the middle of the valley. Beyond him was a great lake.

"Mrs Jones," said the Mayor, "can you make your cat stay there till we have built a dam across the valley, to keep all that water back?"

"I will try," said Mrs Jones. "He mostly sits still if he is tickled under his chin."

So for three days everybody in the town took turns tickling Mog under his chin with hay-rakes. He purred and purred and purred. His purring made big

waves roll right across the lake of flood-water.

All this time the best builders were making a great dam across the valley.

People brought Mog all sorts of nice things to eat, too – bowls of cream and condensed milk, liver and bacon, sardines, even chocolate! But he was not very hungry. He had eaten so much fish.

On the third day they finished the dam. The town was safe.

The Mayor said, "I see now that Mog

is a gentle cat. He can live in the Town Hall with you, Mrs Jones. Here is a badge for him to wear."

The badge was on a silver chain to go round his neck. It said MOG SAVED OUR TOWN.

So Mrs Jones and Mog lived happily ever after in the Town Hall. If you should go to the little town of Carnmog you may see the policeman holding up the traffic while Mog walks through the streets on his way to catch fish in the lake for breakfast. His tail waves above the houses and his whiskers rattle against the upstairs windows. But people know he will not hurt them, because he is a gentle cat.

He loves to play in the lake and sometimes he gets so wet that he sneezes. But Mrs Jones is not going to give him any more yeast.

He is quite big enough already!

A Bed for the Night

There were once four friends who travel-
led about the world singing songs and
playing tunes. They called themselves the
Weevils. The eldest was Zeno Weevil. He
was Greek, and he played a zither. Then
came Ian O'Weevil; he was Irish and
played a harp. Then there was Spiqueneau
Weevil, who was French and played the
triangle. Last and youngest was Dunnoo
Weevil, who was Indian and played a
large drum.

They had an old car, and in this they
drove through the jungles and over the
deserts and up the mountains and along
the valleys. Wherever they went, they
sang and played, and people gave them
food or money. And although their car
was so old that it often went wrong,
Dunnoo was so clever that he was always
able to make it go again.

But one winter day when they were

83

crossing a frozen river in very wild country, the ice broke under them, and their car slowly sank down through the cold water until it was gone. The four friends only just managed to escape with the zither, the harp, the triangle, and the drum.

What could they do now?

The wind was blowing and the snow was snowing, and the nearest town was miles and miles away. Night was coming too – the sky was growing darker and darker.

By the side of the river was a crane's nest, piled high with dry reeds and rushes and lined with soft, downy feathers. It looked very snug and comfortable. But when they walked up to it the crane lifted her head with its long, sharp beak, and hissed at them:

"Kaaaa! Be off with you!"

"Please, kind crane, may we spend the night in your warm nest? We are so cold and wet and hungry!"

84

"What can you do in return?"

"We can sing and play for you."

"That's no use to *me*. I've no room for you," said the crane. "Be off before I peck you."

So they went on up the hill, through deep snow.

Next they came to a bear's cave. The bear, brown and furry and big as a horse, was curled up inside very snug on a bed of dried leaves. When he heard the four friends coming he growled fiercely at them.

"Please, kind bear, may we spend the night in your warm cave? We are so cold and wet and hungry and tired!"

"What can you do in return?"

"We can sing and play for you."

"Grrr! Certainly not!" said the bear. "Besides, you might steal my nuts. Be off, before I bite you."

So the four friends went on up the hill. It was growing darker and darker.

Next they came to a little wooden house.

"Thank goodness!" said Zeno. "Whoever lives here will give us a bed for the night." So they knocked at the door.

A dog began to bark angrily and a little old man opened the door. He was not at all pleased to see them.

"Please, kind sir, may we spend the night in your warm house? We are so cold and wet and hungry and tired and thirsty."

"What can you do in return?"

"We can sing and play for you."

"What do I care for that?" said the old man. "I have only one bed, and one chair, and one egg, which I am going to boil for my supper. There is no room for *you*."

And he slammed the door.

The four friends turned sadly away.

Outside the little house was a well, with a bucket hanging in it. They were so thirsty that Ian said, "At least the old man won't grudge us a drink of his water." And he began pulling up the bucket. "My word, it's heavy!" he said.

Just as he pulled the bucket up to the top, the old man's dog ran at them, barking, and knocked over the bucket. Out of it rolled something round and white, and bigger than a football. Before they had time to see what it was, it rolled off down the hill.

The old man put his head out of the door.

"Be off!" he shouted. "Clear out of my garden before I come out with my gun."

So the four friends hurried away.

When they came to the very top of the hill they saw a strange sight.

There was a little house on one leg. The leg was yellow and scaly, like a chicken's claw, and the house was all covered with feathers. When they knocked at the door a little old woman opened it and looked down at them.

"Well," she said, "what do *you* want?"

"Please, kind lady, may we spend the night in your warm house? We are so cold and wet and hungry and thirsty and miserable!"

"What can you do in return?"

"We can sing and play for you."

"That's not enough," she said. "If you can find the egg that my house laid today, and that somebody stole while I was asleep, then you can have a bed for the night."

"What does the egg look like?"

"It is round and white and as large as the harvest moon and I was going to

88

boil it for my supper."

"I know where it is!" said Dunnoo. "The old man must have stolen it and hidden it in his bucket. It went rolling down the hill. We will find it for you."

So they went quickly down the hill again. When they passed the old man's house he shook his fist at them but he did not come out. The moon had risen, and they could see the track in the snow where the egg had rolled downhill.

As it rolled, the snow stuck to the egg and it became bigger and bigger, bigger and bigger, bigger and BIGGER, till it was like a huge snowball. It rolled right into the bear's cave, waking him, and breaking all his nuts. Just as he threw it out in a rage, the four friends came by.

"It was you, was it," growled the bear, "who rolled a snowball into my cave, and broke my nuts and scattered my leaves and woke me? Just wait till I get my paws on you!"

He would have rushed at them, but

Ian quickly stuck his harp into the doorway of the cave, where it just fitted. All the bear could do was to scrape his long claws across the strings, and this made such a sweet sound that soon his head began to nod and his eyes to close.

"Hush!" whispered Ian. "He'll soon fall asleep again. You go on and I will stay here to soothe him." And he began to sing very softly to the bear.

So the other three ran on down the hill.

The big snow-wrapped egg had rolled on, crashing right into the crane's nest and knocking it into the river.

The crane was furious.

"It was you, was it, you wretches," she croaked, "who rolled that ball into my nest? Just wait till I get at you!"

And she spread her wide wings and came at them with her long, sharp beak. But Spiqueneau jumped to one side and held out his triangle so that she flew right into it and stuck fast.

"Quick!" he said to the others. "Go

along beside the river and see if you can find the egg."

And he began tickling the crane under her chin, and singing a little song to soothe her.

The other two ran along the river bank and, thank goodness, there was the crane's nest floating, with the old woman's egg in the middle of it. Zeno reached out with his zither and Dunnoo reached out with his drumsticks, and they just managed to catch the nest and bring it to the bank.

They put the nest back on a dry spot. Then Spiqueneau let the crane out of the triangle. She climbed crossly back on to her nest and began putting it to rights. She was so busy that she took no more notice of the three friends, who hurried back up the hill. When they reached the cave, the bear was fast asleep, so Ian took his harp out of the doorway and helped to carry the egg. It seemed to grow heavier and heavier as they toiled up the hill.

When they passed the old man's house he had gone to bed without any supper.

At last they came to the old woman's house on its yellow leg and they knocked at the door.

The old woman looked out.

"Well?" she said. "Have you found my egg?"

"Yes, here it is!"

"Ah, but is it cracked?" she said. "Wipe off the snow so that I can see."

When they wiped the snow off, there was a big crack. As they looked, it grew longer and longer until the egg fell in half. And out stepped another house on one leg, just like the old woman's.

"I can't eat *that* for my supper," said the old woman, and she went inside her own house.

"But you promised us a bed for the night!"

"Well?" said the old woman. "What are you grumbling about? Now you have a whole *house* of your own!"

And she slammed her front door.

The Weevils were so happy that they began to play and sing. And their little house danced gaily about on its one leg. Then they climbed inside and went to bed.

And next day their house went hopping along with them, over the mountains and the valleys and the plains, wherever they wanted to go.

94

The Patchwork Quilt

Far in the north, where the snow falls for three hundred days each year, and all the trees are Christmas trees, there was an old lady making patchwork. Her name was Mrs Noot. She had many, many little three-cornered pieces of cloth – boxes full and baskets full, bags full and bundles full, all the colours of the rainbow. There were red pieces and blue pieces, pink pieces and golden pieces. Some had flowers on, some were plain.

Mrs Noot sewed twelve pieces into a star. Then she sewed the stars together to make bigger stars. And then she sewed *those* together. She sewed them with gold thread and silver thread and white thread and black thread.

What do you suppose she was making?

She was making a quilt for the bed of her little grandson Nils. She had nearly finished. When she had put in the last

95

star, little Nils would have the biggest and brightest and warmest and most beautiful quilt in the whole of the north country – perhaps in the whole world.

While his granny sewed, little Nils sat beside her and watched the way her needle flashed in and out of the coloured pieces, making little tiny stitches.

Sometimes he said,

"Is it nearly done, Granny?"

He had asked her this question every day for a year. Each time he asked it, Mrs Noot would sing,

> "Moon and candle
> Give me your light,
> Fire in the hearth
> Burn clear, burn bright.
>
> Needle fly swiftly,
> Thread run fast,
> Until the quilt
> Is done at last.
>
> The finest quilt
> That ever was,

Made from more than
A thousand stars!"

This was a magic song, to help her sew quickly. While she sang it, little Nils would sit silent on his stool, stroking the bright colours of the quilt. And the fire would stop crackling to listen, and the wind would hush its blowing.

Now the quilt was nearly done.

It would be ready in time for Nil's birthday.

Far, far to the south of Mrs Noot's cottage, in the hot, dry country where there is no grass and it rains only once every three years, a wizard lived in the desert. His name was Ali Beg.

Ali Beg was very lazy. All day he slept in the sun, lying on a magic carpet, while twelve camels stood round it, shading him. At night he went flying on his carpet. But even then the unhappy camels were not allowed to sit down. They had to stand in a square, each with a green lamp hanging on a chain round its neck, so that when Ali Beg came home he could see where to land in the dark.

The poor camels were tired out, and very hungry too, because they never had enough to eat.

As well as being unkind to his camels, Ali Beg was a thief. Everything he had was stolen – his clothes, his magic carpet, his camels, even the green lights on their necks. (They were really traffic lights; Ali Beg had stolen them from the city of Beirut one day as he flew over, so all the traffic had come to a stop.)

In a box Ali Beg kept a magic eye which could see all the beautiful things everywhere in the world. Every night he looked into the eye and chose something new to steal.

One day when Ali Beg was lying fast asleep, the eldest of the camels said, "Friends, I am faint with hunger. I must have something to eat."

The youngest camel said, "As there is no grass, let us eat the carpet."

So they began to nibble the edge of the carpet. It was thick and soft and silky. They nibbled and nibbled, they munched and munched, until there was nothing left but the bit under Ali Beg.

When he woke up he was very angry.

"Wicked camels! You have ruined my carpet! I am going to beat you with my umbrella and you shall have no food for a year. Now I have all the trouble of finding another carpet."

When he had beaten the camels, Ali Beg took his magic eye out of its box.

He said to it:

"Find me a carpet
Magic Eye,
To carry me far
And carry me high."

Then he looked into the magic eye to see what he could see. The eye went dark, and then it went bright.

What Ali Beg could see then was the kitchen of Mrs Noot's cottage. There she sat, by her big fireplace, sewing away at the wonderful patchwork quilt.

"Aha!" said Ali Beg. "I can see that is a magic quilt – just the thing for me."

He jumped on what was left of the magic carpet. He had to sit astride, the way you do on a horse, because there was so little left.

"Carry me, carpet,
Carry me fast,
Through burning sun,
Through wintry blast.

With never a slip
And never a tilt,
Carry me straight
To the magic quilt."

The piece of carpet carried him up into the air. But it was so small that it could not go very fast. In fact it went so slowly that as it crept along, Ali Beg was burned black by the hot sun. Then, when he came to the cold north country where Mrs Noot lived, he was frozen by the cold.

By now night had fallen. The carpet was going slower and slower and slower – lower and lower and lower. At last it sank down on a mountain top. It was quite worn out. Ali Beg angrily stepped off and walked down the mountain to Mrs Noot's house.

He looked through the window.

Little Nils was in bed fast asleep. Tomorrow would be his birthday.

Mrs Noot had sat up late to finish the quilt. There was only one star left to put in. But she had fallen asleep in her chair, with the needle halfway through a patch.

Ali Beg softly lifted the latch.

He tiptoed in.

Very, very gently, so as not to wake Mrs Noot, he pulled the beautiful red and blue and green and crimson and pink and gold quilt from under her hands. He never noticed the needle. Mrs Noot never woke up.

Ali Beg stole out of the door, carrying the quilt.

He spread it out on the snow. Even in the moonlight, its colours showed bright.

Ali Beg sat down on it. He said,

"By hill and dale,
Over forest and foam
Carry me safely,
Carry me home!"

Old Mrs Noot had stitched a lot of

102

magic into the quilt as she sewed and sang. It was even better than the carpet. It rose up into the air and carried Ali Beg south, towards the hot country.

When Mrs Noot woke and found her beautiful quilt gone, she and little Nils hunted for it everywhere, but it was not in the kitchen – nor in the woodshed – nor in the forest – nowhere.

Although it was his birthday, little Nils cried all day.

Back in the desert, Ali Beg lay down on the quilt and went to sleep. The camels stood round, shading him.

Then the youngest camel said, "Friends, I have been thinking. Why should we keep the sun off this wicked man while he sleeps on a soft quilt? Let us roll him on to the sand and sit on the quilt ourselves. Then we can make it take us away and leave him behind."

Three camels took hold of Ali Beg's

clothes with their teeth and pulled him off the quilt. Then they all sat on it in a ring, round the star-shaped hole in the middle. (Luckily it was a *very* big quilt.)

The eldest camel said,

"Beautiful quilt,
So fine and grand,
Carry us home
To your native land."

At once the quilt rose up in the air, with all the camels sitting on it.

At that moment, Ali Beg woke. He saw them up above him. With a shout of rage, he jumped up and made a grab for the quilt. His fingers just caught in the star-shaped hole.

The quilt sailed along with Ali Beg hanging underneath.

The youngest camel said, "Friends, let us get rid of Ali Beg. He is too heavy for this quilt."

So all the camels humped and bumped and thumped, they knocked and

rocked, they slipped and tipped, they
wriggled and jiggled, until the needle
which Mrs Noot had left sticking through
a patch ran into Ali Beg's finger. He
gave a yell and let go. He fell down and
down, down and down and down, until he
hit the sea with a great SPLASH.

And that was the end of Ali Beg.

But the quilt sailed on, with the

camels. As they flew over Beirut, they threw down the twelve green traffic lights.

When at last they landed outside Mrs Noot's house, Nils came running out.

"Oh, Granny!" he cried. "Come and see! The quilt has come back! And it has brought me twelve camels for a birthday present."

"Dear me," said Mrs Noot, "I shall have to make them jackets, or they will find it too cold in these parts."

So she made them beautiful patchwork jackets and gave them plenty of hot porridge to eat. The camels were very happy to have found such a kind home.

Mrs Noot sewed the last star into the patchwork and spread the quilt on Nils's bed.

"There," she said. "Now it's bedtime!"

Nils jumped into bed and lay proudly under his beautiful quilt. He went straight to sleep. And what wonderful dreams he had that night, and every night after, while his granny sat in front of the big fire, with six camels on either side of her.